Olive Oh

Gets Creative

By Tina ... Tiff Bartel

Book design by Sarah Taplin
Illustrations by Tiff Bartel

Published in the United States by Jolly Fish Press, an imprint of North Star Editions, Inc.

First Edition
Second Printing, 2021

This is a work of fiction. Names, characters, places, and incidents are either the product of the author's imagination or are used fictitiously, and any resemblance to actual persons living or dead, business establishments, events, or locales is entirely coincidental.

Library of Congress Cataloging-in-Publication Data (pending)
978-1-63163-567-0 (paperback)
978-1-63163-566-3 (hardcover)

Jolly Fish Press
North Star Editions, Inc.
2297 Waters Drive
Mendota Heights, MN 55120
www.jollyfishpress.com

Printed in the United States of America

Table of Contents

All About Olive Oh

Hi! I'm Olive Sun-Hee Oh. I live in Los Angeles, California. Right now I'm in third grade, but I am going to be a professional artist one day.

Here are some of the most important facts about me:

- I got my middle name, Sun-Hee, from my grandma. She's an amazing knitter, and she makes me the coolest hats.

- My mom, Julie, works as an interior designer, which is like being an artist for people's homes.

- My brother, Ray, is in sixth grade. He loves K-pop and is a pretty good dancer.

- My sister, Shelly, is in ninth grade. She's going to be a doctor one day, like our dad was.

- My dad died before my first birthday. I don't remember him since I was so little, but Shelly and Ray tell me he was the best dad ever. We keep a photo of him by the door so we can wave hello and goodbye as we come and go.

- My best friend, Marcus Wong, is the bestest friend you could ever have. We've known each other since kindergarten. That's a long time!

Other fun facts about me:

- I love the color red because it's so bright and pretty. And green, because it makes me feel calm. And blue, because it reminds me of the ocean. Also yellow, orange, and purple—I love purple! You've probably guessed it by now: I have a LOT of favorite colors.

- My favorite food is sujebi soup. It's my grandma's specialty because it's made with lots of Halmoni Sarang. (That means "Grandma Love.")

- What's the most interesting thing about me? My freckles! My freckles are special because they look like a constellation. On my nose, you can find the Big Dipper, which is a pattern of stars that look like a ladle. Pretty cool, huh?

Chapter 1

Today is going to be a spectacular day! Why, you ask? Well, I'm not exactly sure, but my teacher, Mrs. Bramble, told our class that she'll be making a special announcement today. I'm sure it will be great because 1) Mrs. Bramble is an awesome teacher, so I know the announcement will be awesome too, and 2) I found my lucky red beret.

I lost my hat a few weeks ago, but I found it yesterday while cleaning out my closet. Mom told me I had to organize my closet because it's "Spring

Cleaning" and wouldn't it be nice if I participated this time? And what do you know? My red beret was stuck underneath all the toys I never play with anymore!

I'm in my room, fluffing out my beret as best as I can before I go to school, and especially before Grandma sees me wearing it. She's the one who made it for me. In fact, she's made me five hats already. She is a talented knitter. The beret is my favorite though. Mom told me berets are popular in France, especially among artists. I was happy to hear that. One day I'm going to have my picture taken for an art magazine. I'll wear my red beret, and everyone will say, "Hey, that's Olive Sun-Hee Oh! She's a famous artist!"

From the living room, I hear my sister Shelly say, "Come on! We're going to be late!" A second later, I hear loud footsteps running down the hall past my room. It's my brother, Ray. My brother's footsteps are *very* loud. He's twelve years old and already taller than all of us. Mom says it's because he takes after Dad, who was very tall (and according to Mom, had loud footsteps as well).

Dad died when I was just a baby, but we keep a photo of him in a picture frame by the door so we can wave to his smiling face as we come and go. Like today on our way to school. I put on my beret and my backpack and run after Ray.

"Wait for me!" I yell. I try to catch up to my brother, but my legs aren't long enough or fast enough.

Shelly and Ray are putting their shoes on when I reach them.

They look at Dad's picture and say quickly, "Good morning, Appa! See you later, Appa!"

"Hey! What about me?" I yell out the front door. My brother and sister make a run for the school bus waiting outside. Their schools are right across from each other, so they take the bus together. I go with Mom because my school is on the way to her office.

"Mom's running late again," Shelly says with a wave. "Bye, Olive!" With that, she hops on the bus. Ray waves at me from his seat by the window. He also sticks his tongue out. I shake my head at him but then do the same. Ha! Good thing Shelly didn't see us, because she'd definitely give us a lecture about *behaving like children*. But I am a child, so I think it's fine.

"Your face will get stuck that way, Olive."

I spin around. Oops. Grandma is shaking her head, but I can see she's trying to hide a smile.

"Good morning, Halmoni!" I say.

My grandma is sitting in her wheelchair at the dining table, having breakfast. "Did you finish all your homework and reading?" she asks.

I nod. Then I remember something. "Grandma, look!" I point to my beret. "I found it!"

Grandma laughs. "I knew you would. Maybe you could help your mother find her papers so you won't be late for school."

Mom! I run back down the hall to my mom's bedroom. The door is closed. I knock loudly.

"Mom! Are you ready? Today is a special day. I can't be late!"

I hear rustling—and then a crash!

"Umma?" I open the door a teeny, tiny bit. Mom is on the floor, picking up papers and small squares of wood samples. It's really fun when she brings wallpaper samples home for her interior design job, because when she's done with a project, she lets me keep them to make a collage.

"Mom? Are you okay?"

She gathers all her things, stuffs them into her briefcase, and snaps it shut. "I'm ready!" she says with a big smile. "Let's go!"

"Yay!"

As we leave her room, Mom asks, "Olive, how did you get ready so fast today?"

"I have mastered the art of getting ready for school," I say.

Lately I've been getting ready lightning fast. This

morning I chose my outfit in the blink of an eye: purple polka-dot overalls with a yellow zebra-striped T-shirt. Isn't that a creative combination? Sometimes I don't even brush my hair because I think it looks very inspiring that way.

Mom gives me a look that says she doesn't believe me. As we walk by my room, she pokes her head in and gasps.

"Nothing to see here!" I say and quickly shut the door.

You see, the key to getting ready lightning fast is to take everything out of the closet, dump *all* of your clothes on the floor, and *then* choose. Because how else would you be able to visualize the perfect combination?

"Oh, Olive . . ." Mom sighs.

"There's no time to sigh," I say. "We have to go!" I'm glad I have a great excuse to get Mom's mind off my messy room.

"Right!" Mom runs to put her shoes on, and I'm right behind her.

"Bye, Halmoni!" I say to Grandma as I rush past her.

"Have a good day, Olive," Grandma says. "And brush your hair, please! It is very wild today."

Oops. I guess Grandma doesn't find my hair very inspiring. Shelly once told me I have hair like Andy Warhol. He was a famous artist who used lots of bright colors. I love his work. And I'd love to be a famous artist someday. So ever since she said that, I've made it my mission to never brush my hair ever again.

When I'm done tying my shoes, I fix my beret and look up at Dad's picture. "Bye, Appa. See you after school!"

Mom blows him a kiss, and we're out the door.

Chapter 2

I make it to my seat right before the bell rings. Marcus is already in his seat next to mine, with his homework and pencil ready on his desk. He's the best student in class, and I'm proud to be his best friend. Even though I'm not the greatest student (or the best behaved), Marcus is proud to be *my* best friend. We've been friends since kindergarten, so we're almost like siblings. Sometimes I think he's more like my brother than my real brother! He's a lot nicer and more patient than Ray too.

Mrs. Bramble gets up from her chair. "Good morning, class."

"Good morning, Mrs. Bramble," we all say.

Our teacher smiles and asks, "Are you all ready for the big announcement?"

I scream, "YES!"

Everybody in my class looks at me and starts laughing. Even Mrs. Bramble. I can't help but laugh too. What can I say? I can never contain my excitement, especially not in class.

Then everybody starts clapping and *woo-hoo*ing. Mrs. Bramble has to count to five so we all settle down.

I look at Marcus. He is grinning at me, so I know

he's excited too, but his hands are folded on top of his desk. I fold my hands too. If I'm ever in doubt about what I should be doing, I look at Marcus to help me figure it out.

Mrs. Bramble sees me and gives me a nod. I nod back. I want her to know that I didn't *mean* to scream out my excitement and make my entire third-grade class do the same. Thankfully, the other students quiet down and give their attention to Mrs. Bramble.

"Thank you, class. I appreciate your enthusiasm," Mrs. Bramble says. "As you know, every spring, Lakeview Elementary has a school-wide event to celebrate the start of the new season. This year, we're going to have an art show!"

"Yeah!" I say along with my classmates. Even Marcus joins in.

This time, Mrs. Bramble lets us celebrate the news. Ally Leeman, one of my classmates, gets out of her seat and does a spin. She is a jazz dancer and likes to show off her skills. Sometimes at recess, she spins so much that I wonder if she'll get so dizzy that she falls. I know I would!

Right now, though, she does a mini-spin. Then everybody does a spin of their own. Marcus and I get up too. I already know what he's thinking, and he knows what I'm thinking. We take a few steps away from each other and jump toward each other into a high five. Then we fall down laughing. An art show! What a great way to showcase my talent!

"Okay, class. Let me give you some very important information about the show," Mrs. Bramble says. One by one, we all sit down and listen.

"The theme of the show is *Portraits*. Your artwork can be a photo, drawing, painting, or sculpture of a person or a group of people. All the art will be displayed next Friday after school in the auditorium for your family and friends to come see," Mrs. Bramble says.

I can't wait to tell Mom, Grandma, Shelly, and Ray.

Good thing I found my lucky red beret yesterday. Right in the nick of time. I'm going to be bursting with ideas.

"Psst!" I whisper to Marcus.

"What?" he whispers back.

"Do you know what you're going to make?" I ask.

Marcus shrugs. "I'm not sure. What about you?"

"I have lots of ideas. Want me to help you?"

Marcus nods. "That'd be great! Want to come over tomorrow? You can meet our newest cat too!"

"Cool!" I say.

Marcus's dad, Mr. Wong, is a veterinarian. He loves all animals, especially cats. Every once in a while, he'll take Marcus to the animal shelter to pick out a cat to foster until it can get adopted by a forever family. Marcus wants to be a veterinarian one day too. Or a magician. He hasn't decided yet.

"Okay, class, time for homework check," Mrs. Bramble announces.

Marcus and I sit up straight and pay attention. I take out my notebook and try my best not to doodle any ideas for the art show.

Chapter 3

Mom picks me up after school. I don't even wait until I'm inside the car to tell her the news. Afterward, she says, "That's wonderful, sweetheart. If you need any supplies, let me know, and we can pick some up at the Art Barn."

"Thanks, Mom," I say. "But I'm good. I already have a plan." And I do. Actually, I have a lot of plans. So many ideas are swimming inside my head that I don't even notice that we're already parked in the driveway.

Grandma sees us from the living room window and waves one of her knitting needles at me.

"Hi, Grandma!" I yell and run to the front door without waiting for Mom to catch up. When I open the door, Shelly and Ray are on the couch watching TV. Of course, Shelly isn't really watching TV. She's reading a textbook. On the cover is a picture of a swirly ladder. It doesn't look very interesting to me, but Shelly is always reading big books. She wants to become a doctor when she grows up, just like Dad was.

"Guess what?" I announce.

"Chicken butt?" Ray says without taking his eyes off the TV.

"Wrong!" I say as I jump on the couch and squeeze in between him and Shelly. Unlike Shelly, my brother is absorbed by the TV. He's watching a Korean dance competition show. Ray *loves* K-pop dance. He's even in a K-pop dance group with his friends at school. Mom had to give him some ground rules because otherwise he'd practice dancing all day long and forget to do his homework. Even *I* know homework comes first—and I'm younger than him!

Ignoring Ray, Grandma turns around and asks, "What is it, Olive?"

I clear my throat to get Shelly and Ray's attention. "I'm going to have an art show!"

"Oh, is it the school's art show?" Shelly asks, before going back to reading her book. Ray doesn't look impressed by my announcement either.

"We had one too," he says.

My mouth drops. "You did? When?"

Shelly scrunches her nose, trying to remember. "Probably when we were your age."

"Yeah, it's not a big deal," Ray adds.

At this, I stand up with my hands on my hips. I learned that from Mom because that's what she does when she is M-A-D.

"What do you mean it's not a big deal?" I ask. "What if I told you your dance group isn't a big deal, huh?"

"Hey! It's way cooler than an art show!" Ray says.

"Nuh-uh!" I stick my tongue out at Ray and run to Grandma's side. Just then, Mom walks in with a box of her work stuff. She catches a glimpse of Ray and me in our stare down. Oops!

"What's going on?" Mom asks. She drops the box on the floor and puts a hand on her hip. Uh-oh.

My sister turns the page of her book and sighs. Ray and I get into arguments a lot, so today is nothing special. Sometimes I wish Shelly would take her nose out of her book and tell him to be nicer to me. How could Ray say an art show is not a big deal?

I cling to Grandma. I know she'll take my side

because she's always nice to me. Grandma smiles and brushes my hair down. Well, more like *pats* it down, since it's even more tangled than it was this morning.

"Olive and Ray were about to say sorry to each other, weren't you?" Grandma says. I keep my mouth shut and don't look at Mom. I stare at Grandma's lap instead, where an unfinished hat sits next to a ball of yarn. The color is a brilliant blue. It's very pretty. I'm tracing the edge of the hat when Grandma pokes my belly button.

A giggle escapes from me, and my hands fly up to cover my mouth. When I look around the living room to see if anyone heard, Ray groans and finally says, "Sorry, Olive."

Grandma doesn't have to poke my belly button twice for me to say it back.

"I'm sorry, Ray." That's the good thing about my brother and me—whenever we fight, we apologize real fast.

"Phew," Mom says. "Crisis averted!" We all laugh, even Shelly. Mom says this whenever any of us make up after fighting, which is often. Grandma says the three of us fight because we're all very different and we all have big voices. She doesn't mean that we're loud (although I can be). She means that we like to speak up for ourselves, which is okay as long as we don't hurt each other's feelings. But sometimes that does happen, like right now. Oops.

Mom goes into the kitchen and calls out, "Who wants rabokki for dinner?"

"Me!" we all say at once. Even though we're very different, all the Oh siblings love spicy rice cakes with noodles. Yum!

Chapter 4

The next morning, my eyes pop wide open before the sun is up. This never happens, especially not on a Saturday, unless I'm really, really thirsty or really, really excited. Today, I'm really, really excited.

After breakfast, Mom is going to take me to Marcus's house to come up with ideas for the art show. Like Mom always says, two heads are better than one. I wear my red beret just in case we need the extra creative boost.

When I walk into the kitchen, I call out, "Gooooood morning, everybody!"

Mom and Grandma look at me, confused.

"What are you doing up so early?" Mom asks. She is making omelets while Grandma is mixing pancake batter. Yum!

"Just felt like it," I tell Mom. "Did I beat Ray and Shelly?"

Mom narrows her eyes at me. "If you mean did you wake up before them, then yes."

"Oops," I say quickly. "That's what I meant." I take a seat at the dining table. Mom doesn't believe in competition between siblings because she wants us to get along. But how do you get along with your brother and sister *all* the time? It's impossible!

Grandma gives me a wink. She understands. Sometimes I think Grandma is the only person in the world who can understand me. Maybe it's because we share the same name. My middle name, Sun-Hee, is her first name. I think it's very pretty.

When I become a famous artist, I'm going to sign my artwork with my full name. Mom made sure I had a Korean name along with my American name so I wouldn't forget that my family comes from South Korea. I was born in Los Angeles, California, and I've never been anywhere else, but Mom says South Korea is the home of my ancestors. By ancestors, she means the generations and generations of people I'm related to but never had the honor of meeting. According to Mom, family is the most important thing in the world, which is why "there is no competition between siblings." That's a direct quote!

From behind me, I hear a groggy voice say, "Olive, do you have to be so loud this early in the morning?"

It's Shelly. Ray follows behind her like an angry zombie. Oops. I guess I woke them up. Ray rubs his eyes and lets out a big yawn. This makes me yawn too. I guess I'm still a little sleepy.

"Sorry," I tell them as they take their seats in front of me. "I'm too excited for the day."

"You're always excited about something, Olive," Ray says.

I think about this for a moment. My brother is right.

"What can I say? My life is cool!" I say. Mom, Grandma, and Shelly laugh. Ray groans and lays his head down on the table.

"All right," Mom says, bringing over a plate of omelets and pancakes for each of us. "Let's have some breakfast." She nudges Ray to lift his head up.

Grandma brings the carton of orange juice. I pour everyone a glass. I might be loud, but I can also be very helpful. For instance, I look at Mom's omelets. Something is missing. Shelly and Mom reach for their forks, but I say, "Wait!"

"What?" Mom asks.

"Something about these omelets doesn't look right."

Mom, Grandma, Shelly, and Ray stare at their plates and inspect them. They turn the plates this way and that. "What's wrong with them?" Mom asks. "I made sure to cook them all the way so that the cheese melts inside."

"That's not it," I say. I tap my chin with my finger and think. Everybody stares at me.

"Come on, Olive," Shelly says. "We're hungry!"

Then a light bulb turns on inside my head. Instead of telling my family my brilliant idea, I go to the refrigerator and open it. I smile to myself because I am a genius.

Ketchup art!

I take out the ketchup and squeeze a drawing of a bird on Grandma's omelet. It's her favorite animal. Then I draw a ketchup flower on Mom's and a book on Shelly's. For Ray, I draw a funny face with a tongue sticking out. Lastly, I draw a red beret on my omelet. It's perfect because the ketchup is already red.

"Ta-da!" I say when I'm done. Everybody takes a look at each other's omelets.

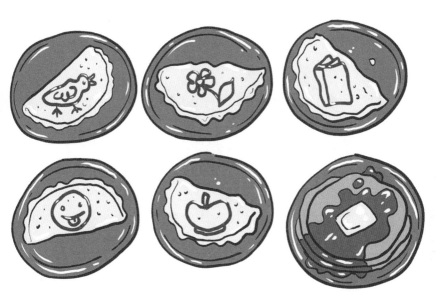

Ray sniffs his. "Looks good, smells good," he says.

Mom nods. "I agree."

"Your drawing skills have improved, Olive," Shelly says.

"Thanks!" I say.

Grandma gives me a big hug. "It's too pretty to eat."

"Yes," Ray says, which is a surprising thing for my brother to say. Then he adds, "But eat we must!" He grabs his fork and gobbles down his entire breakfast in four bites. Did I mention that he is bigger and taller than the rest of us? This is why!

Mom laughs and wipes Ray's cheek with a napkin. "How about the rest of us eat at a normal pace so we don't end up with food on our faces like Ray?"

"Sounds like a plan," I say.

Chapter 5

Mom drops me off at Marcus's house after breakfast.
He lives just a few blocks away from us, so we get there
very quickly. I jump out of the car as soon as it stops,
but Mom calls out, "Olive, you forgot something!"

I already have my backpack with all my art supplies.
She holds up my lunch bag. Only it's not lunch that's
inside. It's banana milk, the most delicious milk in
the world!

"Oh!" I say. "I almost forgot the most important
thing. Thanks, Mom."

Mom leans out the window and gives me the lunch bag. "Have fun. And make sure to use your inside voice."

"I will!" I say.

Unlike our family, Marcus's family is quiet and gets along all the time. That's because Marcus is an only child. I think it must be lonely not having a brother and a sister—even if they make funny faces at you out the school bus window or don't pay attention to you because they are busy becoming a doctor. I'm extra careful not to shout or get overly excited because Mrs. Wong gets headaches after I spend the day with Marcus. I know this because sometimes while I'm over, she'll say, "I need to lie down for a few minutes." Mr. Wong doesn't mind so much because he's busy feeding and caring for his foster cats.

I walk up the steps to the door, but before I can ring the doorbell, Marcus comes out holding a large black cat.

"Wow!" I yell. "That cat is—"

"Shhh!" Marcus shushes me before I can finish my sentence. Oops. At least I'm still *outside* of his house.

"Come on," Marcus says. "I'll introduce you two in my room."

"Okay," I say, following him in. I take my shoes off by the door like we do at my house. Marcus is Chinese

American and I'm Korean American, but both our families have the "no shoes in the house" rule.

"Where are your parents?" I ask as we go upstairs. Marcus waits until we get to the top to answer me. He is having trouble carrying the cat while climbing the stairs. That's how big the cat is!

Finally, he drops the cat in his room and says, "They're outside gardening. My mom told my dad he needs a new hobby. One that doesn't shed fur!"

Marcus and I laugh. The cat jumps on Marcus's bed and twitches its tail.

"I don't think your dad would like anything that doesn't purr!" I say.

"Or doesn't have a tail!" he adds.

"What's the cat's name?" I ask.

Marcus gets up on the bed and holds the cat in his lap. "She doesn't have one yet. Dad can't think of one, and neither can I."

"Hmm," I say. "Can I hold her?"

"Sure," Marcus says. He holds her out to me. The cat lets out the softest, cutest purr. "Hey, she likes you!"

I smile at the cat. "Aww, you are so sweet." I pet her. She has a lot of black fur, but on her back, there are five white dots that zigzag like stars in a constellation.

"I know!" I say. "You can name her Cassiopeia. Look at these dots. They make a constellation!" I point them out to Marcus, drawing lines between them with my finger. "You can call her Cassie for short."

"Cassiopeia," Marcus says. "I like it. Thanks, Olive."

"You're very welcome," I say. Then I remember something. I show Marcus my lunch bag. "This is for you."

Marcus peers inside the lunch bag. "What is it?"

He takes out the two cartons with the words BANANA MILK written on the front.

"My mom bought them from the Korean market. She lets us drink banana milk only on special occasions, but I asked her for permission to share with you," I tell Marcus. "It tastes even better than a real banana! And you can have both as a thank-you for letting me name your cat."

"Cool," Marcus says. "Thanks, Olive, but let's share them."

My eyes open really wide. If someone had given me not one but *two* cartons of banana milk, I'd definitely take both!

"Are you sure?" I ask.

Marcus nods. He gives me a high five. Our hands make a loud smack. Cassie purrs right on cue.

"Did I hear a kitty-cat purr?" Mr. Wong asks, coming into Marcus's room.

"Hi, Mr. Wong," I say. He is wearing a great big

visor on his head. There is dirt on his chin and upper lip, making it look like he has a mustache. I try not to laugh!

"Hello, Olive. I see you've met our newest addition," he says.

"Yes, and named her Cassiopeia!" Marcus says.

"Like the constellation?" Mr. Wong asks.

I nod. Marcus's dad knows all about the stars and the galaxy. When I told him that the freckles on my nose make the shape of the Big Dipper, he brought out a magnifying glass to take a closer look. Now, Mr. Wong's eyes light up as he notices the pattern of the zigzag dots on Cassie's back.

"That is the perfect name," Mr. Wong says as Cassie curls herself around his legs.

"Hey, Olive," Marcus says. "Want to see my idea for the art show?"

"You have an idea for the art show?" I ask. "Already?"

Marcus nods and gets up to grab a large piece of paper from his desk. "This is a rough draft of the photograph I want to take."

We sit on the floor to look at it. The drawing shows him wearing a long cape with a crown on his head. A sash across his chest reads: *Marcus, Animal Rescuer Extraordinaire.*

"I'm thinking of dressing up like this and taking a picture of myself," Marcus says. "Mom said I can use the photo printer!"

The drawing looks wonderful. Marcus looks like a brave and daring king. Most importantly, it's a very creative idea that he came up with. And he didn't even need me or my red beret.

"So, what do you think?" Marcus asks me. He and his dad look at me.

"That's a great idea, Marcus," I say. "I can't believe you already know what you're going to do for the art show."

Marcus shrugs. "I didn't think it would come to me so quickly, because I'm not artistic like you. I guess I was inspired by Cassie and fostering."

Mr. Wong beams at Marcus. Then he turns to me and says, "Isn't that wonderful? Mrs. Wong and I can't wait to see his photograph next week. I also can't wait to see what you have planned, Olive. I know it'll be amazing."

"Definitely," Marcus says. "I bet Olive's artwork is going to wow everybody!"

Will it? I feel a little flutter in my stomach. I remind myself that I have my red beret and all the ideas that are swirling around in my head.

"I can't wait for you and Mrs. Wong to see my work too," I say. "It's going to be terrific!"

"Okay, you two," Mr. Wong says. "If you need me, I'll be in the backyard."

Chapter 6

Marcus and I head downstairs to search for the perfect cape and crown. Cassie has perched herself on the couch. She is taking a snooze.

"According to my sketch, the cape has to be wide enough to tie around my neck," Marcus says.

We both peer at the drawing once more. It's a very good drawing. Maybe even better than my drawings. Suddenly, a funny thought bubbles up in my head. *Is Marcus a better artist than me?*

I shake my head. It doesn't matter, because Marcus Wong is my BFF. I'm proud that he is so talented at drawing.

We both look around his house. "How about the tablecloth on the kitchen table?" Marcus asks.

"That's a great idea!" I say. The tablecloth is long and wide, big enough to wrap around him. I help tie it around his neck. The tablecloth comes down to his feet, so I fan it out.

"Ta-da!" Marcus says.

"Wow," I say. "You look like a superhero!"

"Thanks!"

"What about the crown?" I ask. We take another

look at the drawing. It has to be big enough for his head and have a triangular point at the top.

Suddenly, I have an idea. "I know!" I grab my backpack and flip it over. All of my things fall out in a clutter. Good thing Mr. and Mrs. Wong are still in the backyard.

"Whoa," Marcus says. "What is all that?"

My sketch pad, paint set, tape, and scissors are dumped on the floor. I also have thirty-six markers, three kinds of glitter glue, and a bundle of wallpaper samples Mom gave me from her work. I reach for the wallpaper samples. The papers are all shapes and sizes, with a variety of patterns—lines, circles, and even flowers!

"We can tape the pieces together to make your crown," I say happily.

"Hey, that's awesome!" Marcus says.

We get to work. I grab the scissors while Marcus arranges the papers into the shape of a crown. Then we tape the papers together. When we're done, I help Marcus put it on.

"It fits!" I say. In his tablecloth cape and paper crown, Marcus walks over to Cassie. She meows because he has woken her from her catnap. He picks her up gently. Then he jumps on top of the coffee table, which I'm sure isn't allowed. I look out into the backyard through the kitchen window. Mr. and Mrs. Wong are digging through dirt. They look very busy.

"Well?" Marcus asks, watching me.

"The coast is clear!"

Marcus points to the kitchen counter. "Can you use Mom's camera to take a picture of me?"

"Sure." Although my mom takes all her photos on her phone, Mrs. Wong is old-school. She still likes to print pictures and frame them, which is why the Wongs' walls are full of photographs like in an art gallery.

"Okay, Marcus," I say. "Give me your best animal rescuer pose!"

Marcus tilts his head up high, holds Cassie in one hand, and puts the other one on his hip.

Click! Click! Click!

"Marcus, what are you doing on the coffee table?" Mrs. Wong asks, suddenly inside the house.

Uh-oh!

Marcus jumps down quickly, but the tablecloth is so long that he trips on it and falls on the carpet. But as he is falling, he drops Cassie, who screeches really loud and jumps onto Mr. Wong's shoulder.

"Whoa!" Mr. Wong says, wobbling to the side. Mrs. Wong acts fast and holds him up with her hands.

"That was close," I say. "Fast reflexes, Mrs. Wong!" I smile at her, but she doesn't smile back. She's looking at the living room: Marcus tangled in the tablecloth, scraps of paper scattered around him, and my art supplies spread all over the floor. Oops.

"Ouch!" Marcus says, rubbing his knees. He gets up, finally untangled. "I'm okay!" Then he sees Mrs. Wong's face. "I'm sorry, Mom," Marcus says. "Olive helped me with my artwork. Didn't you, Olive?"

"Yes, I did!" I say.

Mrs. Wong is staring at all my stuff lying on the floor. She's probably thinking *What a mess!*, so I say, "Don't worry, Mrs. Wong. It's all under control. Art can be messy, but that's part of the process. I read that in a book by a famous painter. I forget who it was, but in the book, there was a picture of the artist's painting studio, and boy, was it a mess. Messier than my room—and that's saying a lot!"

For some reason, Mrs. Wong doesn't look happy. She just shakes her head.

Mr. Wong clears his throat. "I think what Olive means is that all of this will be cleaned up while we go wash off this dirt, right?"

Marcus and I nod. "Right away!" Marcus says.

"Okay," Mrs. Wong says. "And no more jumping off tables, Marcus."

"Yes, ma'am!" Marcus says. This makes Mrs. Wong shake her head even more, but she is laughing now.

"I think Olive brings out the silliness in you, sweetheart," Mrs. Wong says. "Olive, I told your mom you can stay for dinner, if you'd like. It's pizza night."

Marcus and I look at each other. "Yeah!" we say. We forget to use our inside voices, but Mr. and Mrs. Wong laugh.

"Consider it a treat for a job well done," Mr. Wong says.

I'm so happy that I forget that I haven't even started on my artwork. I don't worry though. I know I'll have a grand idea when I least expect it. It's all part of the process!

Chapter 7

On Monday, everybody at school is talking about the art show. I still haven't gotten my idea yet, but there's time. Plus, I feel my creativity brewing. I've been wearing my red beret for four days straight!

When Mrs. Bramble gives us time to work on our artwork, I open up my sketchbook to draw. With my pencil, I write PORTRAITS at the very top.

"Hey, Olive," Ally says. She is carrying a glass jar filled with water. Several paintbrushes are sticking out of it.

"Hi, Ally," I say. "Are you painting?"

"Yeah," she says. "I'm making a watercolor portrait of myself as a jazz dancer!"

"Awesome," I tell her. I wonder if I should do a watercolor portrait, but I don't want to copy Ally. I want to be completely original.

She looks at my sketchbook. "Do you know what you're doing yet?"

I try to cover the blank page. It's okay if she sees it since nothing is there, but I also feel like I'm kind of behind.

So I say, "It's all coming along!" even though that's not really true. My stomach feels fluttery again.

Marcus comes up to my desk with Louis, Cory, and Greta. They are holding pencils, markers, brushes, and pastels in their hands. Cory even has smudges on his T-shirt. I guess he's been working hard on his artwork.

"Hi, Olive," Louis says. "What have you got there?" He tries to grab my sketchbook, but I slam it shut and put it inside my desk.

"Top secret!" I say.

"Wow," Greta says. "It must be really good if it's top secret."

I force a smile. "It is. I've got tons of ideas! There are so many that I can't choose yet."

Oh no. I just lied *again*. I didn't mean to. It just popped out! Now my stomach is really fluttery, like there are a hundred birds in there flapping their wings.

Marcus says, "Olive is going to create something super-duper. She already helped me with my artwork."

"She did?" Cory says. "What's your artwork?"

"It's a self-portrait of me as an animal rescuer," Marcus says.

"Cool!" Louis says. "I'm drawing a portrait of my dog, Henrietta. I'm going to give it to her for her tenth birthday!"

"Wow. That's a great idea," I say. "What about you, Cory and Greta? What kind of portraits are you going to make?"

Greta says, "I'm using pastels to draw all the teachers I've had since kindergarten because I miss them!"

"Is Mrs. Bramble going to be in your drawing?" I ask.

"Of course," Greta says. "She's the best!"

Cory says, "I'm making a clay sculpture of the bestest Greek god ever, Zeus!"

"A sculpture?" I say. I can't believe it. Why didn't I think of that?

"All right, everybody. Time to clean up and take your seats, please," Mrs. Bramble says at the front of the classroom. "Did you all make progress on your art pieces?"

"Yes!" my classmates answer. I don't say anything

though. I don't have a clue what I'm going to make for the art show. I take off my beret and stare at it.

I'm beginning to think that my lucky hat isn't so lucky.

Chapter 8

"How was school, Olive?" Grandma asks when I get home. Mom dropped me off and is headed to a work event. She knew right away when I got in the car that I was *not* my usual self, which is nonstop talking. I told her I didn't feel like talking today, so she let me listen to Ray's K-pop playlist. It was okay.

I walk over to Grandma. She is sitting in front of the living room window.

"What's wrong?" she asks.

"Nothing," I say, but I pick up her knitting needles and yarn and play with them.

Grandma wraps her arms around my waist. "You are getting so big! Soon you'll be bigger than me."

I don't say anything to that. I have lost all my words. I didn't think that could ever happen!

Grandma pokes my side, but I don't giggle this time. I touch the beret on my head instead. Nothing happens. Maybe my hat is broken. Maybe that's why I'm not creative anymore!

"Hello, is Olive here?" Grandma says.

She pretends to knock on my arm. It's kind of funny,

but I don't laugh. I'm still thinking about Cory's sculpture, Greta's pastel drawing, and everyone else's wonderful artwork. Mine would be wonderful too, if only I knew what to create.

"Okay, I see you don't feel like telling Halmoni what's wrong," Grandma says. "So I'll tell you about my day."

"Okay," I finally say.

"Today I saw two bunnies racing on Mr. Garcia's lawn. Right over there." She points across the street. "They were in a race to catch a squirrel, but a dog the size of a bear came running! Then, another dog even bigger than that! Two times the size of a bear!"

I turn to look at her. "Did that really happen, Grandma?" I think she might be telling me a story rather than what *really* happened.

"I promise," Grandma says. "I do not lie. Guess what else I don't lie about?"

"What?" I ask.

"Everything is going to be okay," she says. "Do you believe me?"

I shrug. "Maybe."

Even Grandma's words are not enough to make me feel better, so I go to my room. I lay on my bed, take off my beret, and before I know it, I'm throwing it across the room! It lands on top of all my clothes like a big red ball.

Good riddance to you, red beret. You are no help to me!

I feel kind of bad, so I look up at my ceiling and count sheep. Mom always says a good night's sleep is the best medicine. Maybe a nap will work the same.

I'm almost asleep when I hear loud music. It's coming from Ray's bedroom. Ugh! I jump off my bed and barge into his room.

Ray is practicing a dance routine while watching a K-pop video on his computer. He doesn't see me standing with my hands on my hips.

"Excuse me!" I yell at the top of my lungs.

Ray nearly falls over as he turns around. "Olive, you scared me!"

I march over to his computer and close the screen.

"Hey! You can't do that!" he yells.

"Your music is so loud! I can't think!" I yell back.

Then, before he can yell some more, I jump onto his bed and pull the cover over my head. I am so mad I think I might cry.

"Hey," Ray says in his normal voice. "What's wrong?"

I don't come out from under the cover, but I do answer him. "I'm not a real artist."

"What do you mean?" Ray asks. I can tell he is sitting on the bed now because I feel it move.

"I don't know what to do for the art show," I say. "I know it's not a big deal to you, but it is to me." And all of a sudden, I start to cry.

"Hey, Olive," Ray says. "I've been meaning to apologize to you for saying that. I really am sorry. I didn't mean it. I think you're very talented."

I poke my head out from under the blanket a tiny bit. "Really? You think so?"

"Yeah," Ray says. "You're the most creative person I know."

"Thanks, Ray. You're the best dancer in the whole world!"

Ray laughs. "Thanks, but do you know every person in the whole world?"

I shake my head. "It doesn't matter because I just know!"

Right then, Shelly walks by the room and stops in the doorway. "What are you guys doing?"

"We're thinking of what Olive could make for the art show," Ray says.

"You're going to help me?" My eyes open so wide I think they're going to pop out!

"Sure!" Ray says. "Want to help, Shel?"

"Sure," she says. "I'm done with the extra Physio reading, so I have time."

I don't know what Physio is, but I'm sure glad my sister and my brother have time to help me!

"Let's start with a list in your notebook," Shelly says. "That's how I organize my study plans. It's my secret weapon." I can't believe she just told me a secret!

She tells me to write down my favorite ways of making art. I list my top three:

1. Colored-pencil drawing

2. Collage

3. Painting

Ray asks me what my favorite things are. Of course I write art as number one! Then I write down family and then friends. I still don't know what I'm going to do, but I think this is a good start.

Chapter 9

After Shelly, Ray, and I finish brainstorming, we gather around the dinner table without Mom because she is still at work.

"Wow," Ray says. "Dinner smells delicious!"

Shelly helps Grandma bring all the bowls and side dishes to the dinner table. When Mom isn't home, Shelly takes over for her. Sometimes my sister is bossy, but today she is helpful.

"This is a special soup called sujebi," Grandma says,

passing out spoons and chopsticks for us. "Go ahead, let's eat."

"Jal meok-ge-sseum-ni-da!" Shelly, Ray, and I say. This is how we thank the person who prepared our food. Tonight, we are saying thank you to Grandma.

I breathe in the yummy smell and say, "Ahhh."

Ray is already slurping the hot soup. He takes careful bites of something that looks doughy. I take a bite too. It's so chewy and yummy!

"Do you like it, Olive?" Grandma asks. "It has superpowers."

"Halmoni, soup can't have superpowers!" I say.

"This one does," Grandma says. "It came all the way

from South Korea, where our family is from. When I was a little girl like you, my family did not have a lot of things. We only had each other—and this soup. Almost every night, my mother made us this soup. My father worked very hard. He was very tired when he came home. But at dinnertime, he would drink all of the soup and say, 'I have strength for another day!'"

"I didn't know that, Grandma," Shelly says.

Grandma takes a sip of her soup. Looking at me, she says, "Tonight, I want to give you strength."

I eat the soup slowly so I can savor it. And you know what? I start feeling better. I think Grandma is right. This soup does have superpowers.

Later that night, when I'm getting into bed, Mom

knocks on my open door. She doesn't have to knock,

but she does anyway because my mom is very polite.

Not like Ray—or sometimes me!

"Can I come in?" she asks.

"Of course," I say. "You're my mom!"

She laughs and tucks herself in next to me. "Just checking." She puts her head against mine and asks, "Are you feeling better?"

"Yes," I say. I don't want to lie anymore. It doesn't make me feel good. Plus, I really do feel better now.

"Can you tell me what happened today at school?" Mom asks.

I take a deep breath. I tell her everything, from Marcus being a better artist than I am, to everybody having great ideas for the art show, and even to me getting mad at Ray for his loud music. I talk and talk.

Mom listens the whole time. When I'm finally done talking, I feel a bit better.

"It sounds like a lot has happened today," Mom says. "Thank you for sharing that with me."

"You're welcome," I say. "I'm sorry I didn't tell you earlier. I was not in a good mood."

"Is that why your beret is in the corner on top of all your clothes?" she asks.

I let out a sigh. "I don't think it's so lucky anymore. I used it all up."

Mom turns so we're face-to-face. "You know what I think, Olive?"

"What?"

"I don't think you need a lucky red beret. You are already creative and talented, and you should be proud of who you are," Mom says. "Did I ever tell you about the time you had to stay in the hospital after you were born?"

"Yes, millions of times!" I say, but I sit up to listen to the story again.

Mom laughs and puts her arm around me. "You were very, very small when you were born. The doctors told us you had a weak heart. I had to come home to take care of your brother and sister, but your dad stayed with you the whole time. You had to sleep in a small, clear box called an incubator to help you get well. There was a tiny hole in the side of that box so your dad could hold your tiny hand. And he never let go until you got healthy enough to come home."

"I love that story," I whisper.

"Your dad and I had no doubt you would grow up to have the biggest heart to share with the world. So whatever you do, as long as you do it with your whole heart, it'll be wonderful. And I'll always be proud of you no matter what. I hope you can be proud of yourself too."

I lean against Mom. She is the best mom ever. "I love you, Umma."

She gives me a kiss on top of my head and says, "I

love you too." Then she tucks me in and turns off the light.

Today started off being a not-so-great day, but I'm glad to report that things are looking up! I feel super lucky to have my family. They are the greatest! And I know that they'll always be there for me like they were today.

In fact . . . that gives me the perfect idea for the art show!

Chapter 10

Once I have my idea, the rest of the week goes by in a blur. I spend all day Tuesday and Wednesday working on my project. I fill two sketchbooks with drafts and drawings using different color combinations. But to keep my idea top secret from my family, I tuck all my sketches under my bed. I even make sure not to leave any hint of my artwork on the floor or on my desk. Who knew I could be organized during the art-making process?

Now it's finally the day of the art show! I get ready

lightning fast, but this time I remember to close my door so Mom won't see that my method of getting ready is still not very organized.

Shelly and Ray zoom past me for the front door.

"Bye, Appa! See you later, Appa!" they say as they run out to the school bus. I run after them, but I stop at the doorway.

"Bye, Shelly! Bye, Ray!" I wave to them. They don't seem to hear me even though I'm really loud. I see them get in their seats by the window. Then they look out the window and wave back at me.

"See you later at your art show, Olive!" Shelly says.

"Can't wait to see it, Ol!" Ray shouts.

I'm smiling so big my cheeks hurt. Then I turn back inside and yell, "Mom! Let's go! We're going to be late!"

Grandma is sitting in her usual spot by the living room window, shaking her head. "Some things never change."

We both laugh as Mom walks out of her room. "What's so funny?" she asks.

"Nothing!" I say.

Mom smiles and taps my head. "I see you're wearing your beret again."

I nod. "Even if it's not lucky, it's still my favorite hat because Grandma made it for me."

Grandma gives me a wink. I wave goodbye and tell

her I'll see her at school. I'm so excited for the show, I don't know how I'll get through the morning!

All day long, I fidget and stare at the clock above the whiteboard. Even Marcus stares at it. In fact, I think the whole class watches the clock, waiting for the art show. Finally Mrs. Bramble says, "Okay, class, it's showtime!"

Woo-hoo! We get in a line to walk to the auditorium. My family will be here soon! I turn around to face Marcus, who's standing behind me. He looks worried.

"Marcus, are you okay?" I ask.

"Um, not really," he says.

"What's wrong?" I ask.

Marcus stares at the floor and whispers, "I'm scared that my artwork isn't very good. What if everyone's is better than mine?"

"Marcus," I say. "Don't worry. You made your portrait because you love rescue animals, right?"

"Yes," he says.

"Then your portrait is already great because it came from the thing you love."

Marcus scratches his head. "I never thought of it like that. Thanks, Olive."

We high-five. "That's what best friends are for!"

"Okay, class," Mrs. Bramble says. "We're heading over to the art show."

"Yeah!" we cheer.

When we enter the auditorium, the walls are filled with all kinds of art. All the classes at Lakeview Elementary turned in their artwork yesterday, including ours. Our teachers must have put them up after school. Some art that can't hang on the walls sits in the center of the auditorium. Everyone did a fantabulous job! I feel like I'm at a museum.

Teachers and students from other classes start filing in. Mrs. Bramble says, "Class, your artwork is at the front of the auditorium on the wall next to the stage. You should all be very proud of yourselves. You did a wonderful job!"

She also tells us to stay here with our class until our family members come, and not wander off on our own. I'm so giddy, I start to hop from one foot to the other.

"There she is!" I hear from across the room. It's Ray! And Mom, and Grandma, and Shelly! I want to run over to them, but I remember Mrs. Bramble told us we have to wait here. I am a very good listener today.

I wave both of my arms at my family. I wave and wave so much that my beret almost falls off. Oops!

"Congratulations on your very first art show, sweetheart," Mom says. I feel myself blush. I can't believe I'm in an art show! She and Grandma take turns giving me hugs. Shelly and Ray give me high fives.

"Show us your work, Olive," Shelly says.

"Okay!" I look at Mrs. Bramble to get permission to leave our class. "My family is here, Mrs. Bramble!"

She smiles and says hello to everyone. "Have a great time with your family, Olive."

"I'll see you later, Marcus," I say.

"I'll find you when my parents get here," Marcus says. I give him a thumbs-up.

I hold Grandma's hand as we walk toward the front of the auditorium. On the way, I notice a gray statue sitting on top of a table. It's Cory's sculpture of Zeus.

"Look!" I say. "This is my friend Cory's art."

"Wow," Grandma says. "That's very good."

Just then, Cory comes over with his parents. "Hey, Olive!"

"Cory!" I say. "Your sculpture of Zeus is so good."

"Thanks!"

Shelly and Ray look around the room at the paintings, sculptures, and photographs. Some are of famous presidents and musicians. One must be Louis's art because it's a portrait of a Great Dane.

"These *are* good. I think they're better than when I had my art show," Ray says.

I look up ahead and see it: my artwork!

"Are you ready?" I ask my family.

They yell, "Yeah!"

Everyone nearby looks over at us.

"Oops," Mom says. We all laugh. I have the best family.

I run over to my art and stand next to it. "Ta-da!"

After hearing Grandma's story about when she was a little girl and Mom's story about Dad holding my tiny hand, I realized what I wanted to create. I figured out what was in my heart this whole time: my family!

Since the theme of the art show was *Portraits*, I did a colored-pencil drawing of us in our living room. First, I drew Shelly on our couch reading a book. Ray is next to her with his headphones on, listening to music.

Grandma is sitting by the window and knitting. Next to her, Mom is hugging me from behind. I am smiling—and wearing my red beret, of course! A framed photo of Dad is watching over us from above.

It is the most colorful drawing I've ever made. And in the bottom right-hand corner, I signed my name: *Olive Sun-Hee Oh.*

Mom, Grandma, Shelly, and Ray *ooohh* and *ahhh.*

"Olive," Mom starts to say. Then she stops. She reads the label underneath my drawing out loud: "My Family: A Portrait of Love." Mom gives me a big kiss and hugs me so tight I can't breathe.

MY FAMILY: A PORTRAIT OF LOVE

Grandma taps me on the shoulder and asks, "Do I get a hug too?" So I turn around to give her a kiss and a hug.

"You were right, Halmoni," I say. "Everything turned out okay!"

"Better than okay," Shelly says. "This is a great portrait of our family."

"Yeah," my brother says. "We should put it up in the living room. If that's okay with you, Olive."

"Sure!" I say.

Just then, Marcus comes over with Mr. and Mrs. Wong.

"Hello, Olive," Mrs. Wong says to me. "Is this your drawing?" She looks closely at it, very carefully, inspecting it inch by inch. I gulp.

"Yes," I say. "It's a portrait of my family."

Mrs. Wong smiles. "It's beautiful. I love it!"

"Thank you!" I say.

Marcus takes us to see the photograph of him dressed as an Animal Rescuer Extraordinaire. He gets lots of *ooohhs* and *ahhhs* too.

"Your drawing is great, Olive," Marcus says. "I think you're the most creative."

"You know what, Marcus?" I say. "I think we're all creative. Look at the auditorium!"

We take our time looking around at all the art. There are so many different kinds of drawings, paintings, and sculptures.

"I am so very inspired!" I say.

Marcus laughs. "Uh-oh. Whenever you're inspired, you do something that gets you into trouble."

I give him my biggest smile. "What can I say? It's all part of the process!"

The End

Discussion Questions

1. Why does Olive feel worried when she sees Marcus's drawing? Have you ever felt something similar?

2. At the start of the story, Olive is jealous of her friends' ideas. But by the end, she's able to celebrate everyone's art. What changed?

3. Olive's siblings help her make lists to organize her ideas. How would you help someone who was stuck working on a creative project?

4. Both Marcus's photograph and Olive's drawing show what they love. If you created a portrait of something you love, what would you make? Why?

About the Author

Tina Kim spent her childhood dreaming of becoming an artist one day. Somehow she ended up writing about artists instead—and she loves every minute of it. When she is not writing, Tina likes to eat lots of mac and cheese and watch travel documentaries with her dog, Henry. She lives in Los Angeles, California.

About the Illustrator

Tiff Bartel is a multimedia artist, creating work in illustration, design, film, and music. She lives in Winnipeg, Manitoba, Canada with her husband and baby, and their cat and dog.